A Caribbean Work

AUTHOR

Sundiata Gibbs

EDITOR

Roxanne Brancker

(Media Support International Inc.)

ILLUSTRATIONS

Jody Forte

(Media Support International)

EDITORIAL TEAM

Sundiata Gibbs

Teri-Ann Gibbs

Roxanne Brancker

ISBN: 978-976-95873-4-2

1

Dedicated to my inquisitive daughter
Brielle

It was a crisis for children
and adults alike,

the day Santa and his elves
decided to strike.

I remember the day.
I was about ten,

watching the news
breaking on CNN

Santa's lawyers were speaking
and explaining his plight.

How his salary was low
and how money
was tight.

How his sack just got heavier
and he was getting too old.

How he needed a new place,
the North Pole was too cold.

The elves were disgruntled;
Rudolph's nose was dimmer.

And the milk and the cookies
didn't help him get slimmer.

You see, Santa was the only one
left doing this work.

Mrs Clause had left him
and became a store clerk.

The Tooth Fairy had retired
and made a fortune sewing.

The Easter Bunny became Energizer
and kept going and going.

14

So when Christmas Eve came around, tensions were high.

Little boys started to riot; little girls started to cry.

Then Santa felt bad
and he got an idea.

He loaded his sack
and prepared his sleigh.

18

And with a renewed sense of duty,
he set out in flight.

And even the naughty received gifts
that night.

And even though Santa didn't get
what he desired, he decided to do
his job until he got fired.

20

So don't say he is not real.
Don't call him a myth.

To show your appreciation
you should give him a gift.

22

Say nice things about him. Don't scandal his name.

Because you never know when Santa will strike once again.

CPSIA information can be obtained
at www.ICGtesting.com
Printed in the USA
BVRC100522171121
621776BV00003B/68